Dig for Gold
&
Go Rocket!

D1065769

Early ★ Reader

First American edition published in 2021 by Lerner Publishing Group, Inc.

An original concept by Alison Donald
Copyright © 2022 Alison Donald

Illustrated by Jo Byatt

First published by Maverick Arts Publishing Limited

Maverick
arts publishing

Licensed Edition
Dig for Gold & Go Rocket!

Lerner Publications Company
An imprint of Lerner Publishing Group, Inc.
241 First Avenue North
Minneapolis, MN 55401 USA

For reading levels and more information, look up this title at www.lernerbooks.com.

Main body text set in Mikado. Typeface provided by HVD Fonts.

Library of Congress Cataloging-in-Publication Data

Names: Donald, Alison, author. | Byatt, Jo, illustrator. | Donald, Alison. Dig for gold. | Donald, Alison. Go rocket!
Title: Dig for gold ; & Go rocket! / Alison Donald ; illustrated by Jo Byatt.
Other titles: Readers. Selections
Description: First American edition, licensed edition. | Minneapolis : Lerner Publications, 2021. | Series: Early bird stories. Early reader: Pink | "First published by Maverick Arts Publishing Limited."—Page facing title page. | Audience: Ages 4–8. | Audience: Grades K–1. | Summary: "A pirate and his dog dig for treasure, and a scientist's rocket takes him from the store to the park and beyond"—Provided by publisher.
Identifiers: LCCN 2020013937 (print) | LCCN 2020013938 (ebook) | ISBN 9781728417226 (lib. bdg.) | ISBN 9781728420400 (pbk.) | ISBN 9781728418001 (eb pdf)
Subjects: LCSH: Readers (Primary)
Classification: LCC PE1119.2 .D663 2021 (print) | LCC PE1119.2 (ebook) | DDC 428.6/2—dc23
LC record available at https://lccn.loc.gov/2020013937
LC ebook record available at https://lccn.loc.gov/2020013938

Manufactured in the United States of America
1-48980-49233-10/13/2020

EARLY BIRD
STORIES

Dig for Gold
&
Go Rocket!

Alison Donald

Illustrated by
Jo Byatt

Lerner Publications ◆ Minneapolis

The Letter "D"

Trace the lowercase and uppercase letter with a finger. Sound out the letter.

Around,
up,
down

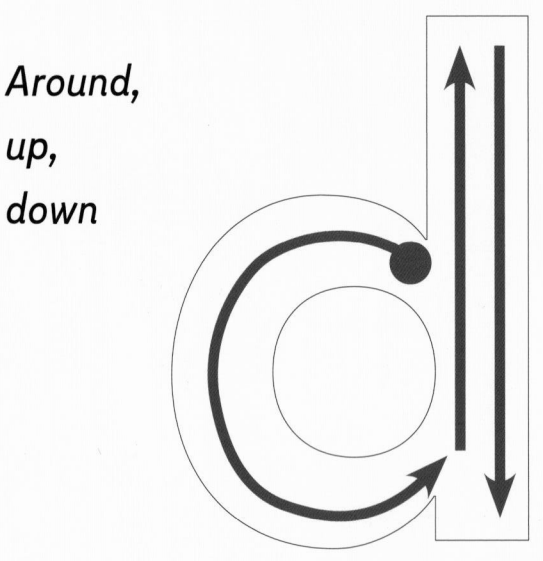

Down,
up,
around

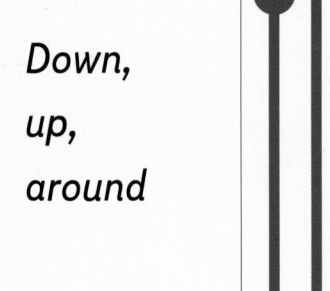

Some words to familiarize:

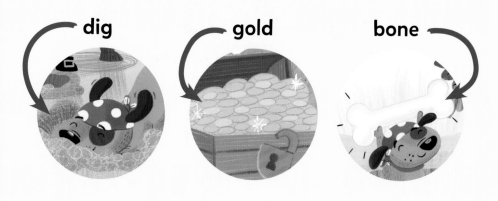

dig   gold   bone

High-frequency words:

a   has   I   to

Tips for Reading *Dig for Gold*

- Practice the words listed above before reading the story.

- If the reader struggles with any of the other words, ask them to look for sounds they know in the word. Encourage them to sound out the words, and help them read the words if necessary.

- After reading the story, ask the reader what Dog digs up at the end of the story.

Fun Activity

Create your own treasure hunt!

Pat has a dog.

Dig for Gold

Dog loves to dig!

Pat has a map.

Pat has a plan.

I love to dig for gold!

Dog has a plan.

Dog has . . .

a bone!

The Letter "B"

Trace the lowercase and uppercase letter with a finger. Sound out the letter.

Down,

up,

around

Down,

up,

around,

around

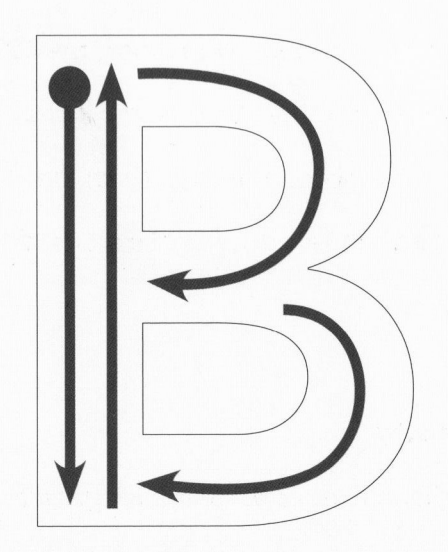

Some words to familiarize:

lab   Bob   store

High-frequency words:

is   at   the   go   up

Tips for Reading *Go Rocket!*

- Practice the words listed above before reading the story.

- If the reader struggles with any of the other words, ask them to look for sounds they know in the word. Encourage them to sound out the words, and help them read the words if necessary.

- After reading the story, ask the reader where Bob went at the end.

Fun Activity

What other places could Bob have gone to with his rocket?

Go Rocket!

Bob is at the lab.

Bob is at the farm.

Bob is at the store.

Bob is at the park.

Up, up, up.

Bob is at the moon!